# Skye Above

ERIC WALTERS

# Skye Above

illustrated by
David Parkins

ORCA BOOK PUBLISHERS

**Library and Archives Canada Cataloguing in Publication**

Walters, Eric, 1957-, author
Skye above / Eric Walters; illustrated by David Parkins.
(Orca echoes)

Issued in print and electronic formats.
ISBN 978-1-4598-0701-3 (pbk.).—ISBN 978-1-4598-0702-0 (pdf).—
ISBN 978-1-4598-0703-7 (epub)

I. Parkins, David, illustrator II. Title. III. Series: Orca echoes
PS8595.A598S555 2014       jc813'.54       C2014-901958-0
C2014-901959-9

First published in the United States, 2014
**Library of Congress Control Number**: 2014936052

**Summary**: Skye's birthday wish comes true when her parents plan a Costa Rican adventure that
includes zip-lining, parasailing and snorkeling.

Orca Book Publishers gratefully acknowledges the support for its publishing programs
provided by the following agencies: the Government of Canada through the Canada Book
Fund and the Canada Council for the Arts, and the Province of British Columbia
through the BC Arts Council and the Book Publishing Tax Credit.

MIX
Paper from
responsible sources
FSC
www.fsc.org  FSC® C016245

*Orca Book Publishers is dedicated to preserving the environment and has printed
this book on Forest Stewardship Council® certified paper.*

Cover artwork and interior illustrations by David Parkins
Author photo by Sofia Kinachtchouk

ORCA BOOK PUBLISHERS          ORCA BOOK PUBLISHERS
PO Box 5626, Stn. B                 PO Box 468
Victoria, BC Canada                Custer, WA USA
v8R 6s4                            98240-0468

www.orcabook.com
Printed and bound in Canada.

17  16  15  14  •  4  3  2  1

# Chapter One

Skye looked out the window of the plane. The clouds were thin and wispy. Below, she could just make out the green rainforest and brown fields. Little towns were visible, joined by black ribbons of roads. The horizon blended with the blue of the ocean. Skye had looked out the window the entire flight. She always did. She loved flying. Loved seeing the changing sky. Even when it was full of clouds, there were so many different types to look at.

Her father sat next to her, watching a movie. Skye had never understood why anybody would rather look at a screen than out the window. You could watch a movie in your living room. Of course,

maybe her father had an excuse. He was a pilot and flew all the time. Her little porthole wasn't much compared to the big cockpit windows he usually looked through.

A dinging sound announced that somebody was going to come on the PA. Skye knew who she wanted it to be.

"Good afternoon, this is your captain."

Skye smiled. Her father gave her hand a little squeeze.

"We will be starting our descent into Costa Rica. I hope you have all enjoyed your flight. It's a beautiful day, and we have a perfect *Skye* above."

Skye laughed out loud.

"Your mother is talking about you again," her father said. "Although I'm sure you're not *completely* perfect... especially when it comes to cleaning your room."

"I cleaned it before we left," Skye said. Her closet, on the other hand, was a different thing completely.

Skye's mother, like her father, was a pilot. It was on a flight that her parents had first met. It was also on a flight that they had gotten engaged. They had flown around the world together. And that's why they knew that when they had a baby, they would name her Skye.

Flying had been part of Skye's life since before she could remember. She traveled with her parents often. Everybody assumed that because both of her parents were pilots, her name was Skye, and she loved to fly, she would someday become a pilot too. Skye thought being a pilot would be great, but what she *really* wanted to be when she grew up was a bird.

Of course, she knew that she couldn't ever *really* be a bird. She'd learned that the hard way when she was five and jumped off the roof of their garage. She had flapped her "wings" as hard as she could. Not only did she not lift off, she didn't even slow down. At least, not until she hit the ground. Her mother told her she was lucky she hadn't broken a leg and made her promise that she wouldn't do it again.

Since she couldn't become a bird, Skye surrounded herself with them instead. Her room was filled with pictures of birds. Her bedspread was covered in birds. She had books about birds. She had little stuffed animal birds. Her family hung bird feeders outside the kitchen window. She had a tree house in the backyard that she called her "nest." Sitting up there, she would sometimes be surrounded by birds that perched on the branches. Best of all, she had two canaries—Zig and Zag—who lived in a big cage in the corner of her room.

Zig and Zag loved to sing and would often wake her up in the morning with their melodies. When she closed the door to her room, they were allowed to fly all around. She liked to pretend that she, too, was a canary. She loved having them as pets, but sometimes she felt bad that Zig and Zag weren't free to fly wherever they liked.

The plane touched down. The landing was so gentle that it felt like the wheels just kissed the runway. People in the plane started to clap. Skye was proud of her mother and clapped along with the rest of the passengers.

# Chapter Two

Skye and her father waited as all the passengers got off the plane. When the plane was empty, all of the flight attendants said goodbye, leaving them to wait for her mother. The captain was always the last person off the plane. Skye was sad that the flight was over but happy to be spending three days on holidays with her parents. She was especially happy because in Costa Rica, the rainforests were filled with exotic birds. Back home, some of the birds had red or blue feathers. Here, the birds were all the colors of the rainbow. Some were so bright they almost glowed. She knew without asking that her parents would be taking her to see some beautiful birds.

Finally, her mother joined them, wearing her captain's uniform and hat. Skye thought that, short of being covered in feathers, it was just about the best thing someone could wear. When she didn't dress like a bird for Halloween, she often dressed as a pilot.

"That was a good landing," Skye said.

"It was. I think I have the best landings of all the pilots in our airline."

"I'd agree with that," her father said. "It was one of the biggest reasons I asked you to marry me."

"I hope there were a few other reasons," her mother joked. She looked at Skye, then back at Skye's father. "So, did you tell her yet?"

Skye's father shook his head. "I wanted us to tell her together."

"Tell me what?" Skye asked.

"We have a surprise for you," her father said.

"Actually, we have more than one surprise for you," her mother added. "Do you remember what

you wished for when you blew out your birthday candles?"

Skye had turned nine the week before.

"Of course I remember," Skye said. "I wanted to fly and fly and fly."

"Well, over the next three days we're going to try to make your wishes come true," her father said.

"But how?"

"If we told you, then it wouldn't be a surprise," her mother said.

"You'll just have to wait, at least until tomorrow, for the first surprise," her father said.

# Chapter Three

The boat burst through another wave, and Skye squealed in delight. She loved rough seas as much as she loved turbulence on a plane. Dozens of people were on board with Skye and her parents. Most of them didn't seem to be enjoying the waves as much as she was.

There were also hundreds of other "passengers" aboard. At Skye's feet was one of six buckets filled with dozens of newly hatched sea turtles. Sixty days earlier, the mother turtles of these endangered babies had crawled up onto the beach and laid eggs. Biologists had protected them when they hatched and had helped them into the sea. Without that help,

only a few of them would have lived through the first day. Most would have been eaten as they crawled across the beach or in the shallow waters of the shore. Now, they would be released into deeper waters, where most would survive.

Skye reached into the bucket and gently picked up one of the babies. Its four limbs, like little paddles, moved frantically.

"Hello, little guy. Don't worry, we're here to help you," she said. "We're taking you out for a swim along with your brothers and sisters. You'll be fine, I promise."

Skye bobbed up and down in the waves with her parents, next to the boat. The boat had looked big before, but out in the middle of the ocean, it seemed small. Skye was even smaller. Everyone wore swim fins and masks. They were ready to snorkel.

Skye had never snorkeled before, but she was a good swimmer. Plus, she had her parents close by. She was ready to be part of the big event.

The first of the buckets was slowly lowered into the water.

"Remember, Skye, you can follow the baby turtles and we'll follow you," her mother said.

"We'll be right there with you," her father said.

"Here we go!" the dive master called out.

He tipped the bucket over, and a flood of baby sea turtles spilled out. Skye took a deep breath and dove down with them. The sea turtles were everywhere. Their legs, like little wings, cut through the water as they raced away. Skye followed one turtle and then another, twisting and turning, diving down and then swimming toward the surface. Brightly colored fish surrounded her, scattering if she came too close. She burst through the surface and took a gigantic breath of air. Her parents came up right beside her.

"Well?" her father asked.

"That felt like flying! I was like a bird gliding through the water."

"You know, that's how a penguin flies," her mother said.

"I'd never thought about that," she said. "Can we keep flying?"

"We're out here for the entire day," her father said. "And look, they're about to release the next batch of baby turtles."

That evening, Skye lay in bed thinking about her day. Her arms were a bit sore, and she could still taste the salt water in her mouth. She had "flown" for a long time, watching all the baby turtles disappear into the depths. There had been colorful clownfish, parrotfish and a big stingray gliding by. She had seen schools of fish change directions in a flash, making it look like they had suddenly changed color too.

There had been schools of minnows that moved like windblown leaves. She had swum with all of them, flying under the surface of the ocean. Skye could only wonder what tomorrow would bring.

# Chapter Four

"Are you excited?" her mother asked.

"Very."

"Are you nervous?" her father asked.

"Just a little. That's what makes it even more exciting. I really want to try it," Skye said.

"And you will," her father said.

Her mother checked the harness one more time to make sure she was safe. Her parents seemed more nervous than Skye was.

"Do you remember the signals?" her father asked.

"This means higher," Skye said as she pointed her thumb up into the air.

"And to go lower and slower?" he asked.

"I remember, but I'll never want to go lower or slower."

Both of her parents smiled. "And to go left and right?"

Skye showed them that she had listened to the instructor. She was ready to go. They had a big family hug and then signaled to the driver and the spotter that they could start. The spotter gave them a big thumbs-up, and the boat slowly started moving forward.

The line between the boat and Skye became taut. The big sail behind her filled with air, and she lifted off the ground. A few feet became a dozen and then two dozen as she floated up into the air. The boat started moving faster. Below her, the sandy beach was replaced by ocean. The boat headed farther and farther from shore, towing Skye along with it. She wondered if this was what it felt like to be a kite.

She wanted to be a kite on a *longer* string, so she signaled the spotter to go higher. He let out more

line, and she rose up into the air. She soared over boats and the endless blue of the ocean. A long line of pelicans came flying by and passed underneath her. Not only was she flying, she was actually flying higher than the birds.

As the boat started to turn, she drifted far off to the side, the full sail holding her up. She pushed on the bar, first left, then right, zigzagging through the air. She wished that her birds Zig and Zag could have been there to fly with her too.

The boat made long, smooth circles, heading out to sea and then back toward the beach. Each time she faced the ocean, Skye felt so happy. She didn't want the flying to end. Finally, the boat neared the beach and slowed to a stop. The sail, still full of air, acted like a parachute and gently dropped Skye down. The sandy beach was beneath her once again. Her parents smiled up at her with open arms. She almost landed right on top of them.

"That was wonderful!" Skye said.

"Was it like flying?" her mother asked.

"Not *like* flying. It *was* flying. It just felt too short!"

"You were up there for almost an hour," her father said.

"Really? It didn't seem that long."

"I'm not surprised. I always find that time flies when you're flying," her father joked.

"That means that tomorrow is going to go past in seconds," her mother added.

Skye could hardly wait to find out how.

# Chapter Five

Skye had had a hard time falling asleep because she was so excited about what was coming next. At first light, she had gotten out of bed to look out the window. The hotel was surrounded by the rainforest, which was home to all kinds of birds. They were already calling out to her with cheeps and chirps, whistles, squawks and songs. People were usually grumpy when they first got up, but birds were different. They always seemed so excited to welcome a new day.

Quietly, so as not to wake her parents, Skye opened the sliding door and stepped out onto the balcony. Their room was high enough in the trees

that it almost felt like a nest. She sang her own song as a greeting to the birds. The day had begun.

* * *

They had been driving for hours, heading inland, away from the ocean. Along the way, they had passed several small villages. Skye had waved to the children going to school, and they had waved back. She wished she could have stopped and played with them. She only spoke a few words of Spanish, but she had traveled around the world and knew that everybody understood a smile.

As they drove on, the paved roads became gravel. The gravel roads became dirt, and the dirt roads became bumpy and narrow. The only thing that stayed the same was that they always seemed to be climbing. The trees became taller and the rainforest thicker, pressing in on both sides and even overhead. It felt like they were driving through a big green living tunnel.

Finally, the driver pulled off the track and parked beside a building.

"We're here," Skye's mother said.

"Where is here?" Skye asked.

"That's all part of the surprise."

Led by their guide, Arturo, Skye and her parents followed a red dirt path into the rainforest. Trees, bushes and vines filled every inch of space. Skye knew there was a clear blue sky and bright sun above them, but she couldn't see more than a glimpse of either. A thick canopy of trees towered over her head.

As she walked, Skye felt like she was passing through a gigantic living thing. And she was. There were lots of plants but also plenty of animals living in the rainforest. She could hear the birds calling out. She also knew there were monkeys, sloths that lazed high in the treetops and big cats such as jaguars and pumas that roamed the forest floor. She figured hundreds of eyes probably watched them as they passed, but she would be lucky to see even a few of them.

A deep, unfamiliar call sounded in the rainforest. "What was that?" Skye asked.

"That was a howler monkey," Arturo said. "Listen." He did a perfect imitation of the monkey. So perfect, in fact, that the monkey answered back. The guide and monkey continued their conversation, calling back and forth to each other.

"What is he saying?" Skye asked.

"Sorry, I only speak English and Spanish," Arturo answered. "But I'd like to think that he's saying good morning and welcoming us to his home."

"Even the animals are friendly in Costa Rica," her mother said with a laugh.

"Do you think he'll come close enough to say hello in person?" Skye asked.

"We'll keep our eyes open," he said. "Maybe we'll be lucky."

As they walked, Skye kept one eye on the rough path and the other on the trees. Even though they hadn't seen a monkey, Arturo kept pointing out other wildlife. There were little flashes of green, blue and yellow in the trees. They saw all sorts of birds, including macaws, budgies and canaries. Skye wondered if the Costa Rican canaries were distant relatives of Zig and Zag. There was a loud crash in the trees, and they all looked up. Skye could see branches moving. "Monkeys!" she cried out.

"Spider monkeys," said Arturo.

They were almost directly above their heads, swinging through the trees. There were four or five of them—no, more! It was a whole troop of monkeys.

"Do you see the baby?" the guide asked.

None of them had. "Come over here and I'll show you." He pointed and Skye tried to follow the line of his arm into the trees. There it was! It was a little brown ball of fur on the back of its much bigger mother. It clung to her as she jumped from one branch to another.

"They live their entire lives up in the trees," Arturo explained. "They travel, eat, sleep and live without their feet hardly ever touching the ground."

They watched as the spider monkeys moved from branch to branch and tree to tree. Often, they held on with one arm or leg—or even their tails—while grabbing the next perch with another limb. Sometimes they just jumped, leaping across open air and landing on another tree. Skye worried that the baby might fall, but he held on tightly. She guessed that monkey parents were just like human parents and wouldn't do anything that was dangerous.

As she looked up, the monkeys seemed to be looking down with interest. Skye wondered if the monkeys had a guide and were observing them in the same way. Finally, the monkeys seemed to get tired of watching and moved on. They swung and jumped from branch to branch until they disappeared from view. Skye continued to listen and could hear them even after she couldn't see them anymore. As they started walking again,

Skye couldn't help thinking that the monkeys' way of traveling looked way more fun.

"Here we are," her mother said.

Skye saw the sign and could hardly believe her eyes—*Hummingbird Feeding Station*! Hummingbirds were her favorite birds in the whole world. She ran forward. Benches lined the sides of the feeding station, along with dozens and dozens of feeders. Skye recognized them because they had the same kind at home. They were colorful clear plastic feeders filled with sugary water. The hummingbirds loved them because the liquid tasted just like flower nectar. They took a seat on one of the benches and waited for the birds to appear. Skye knew that hummingbirds were friendly but also very shy. They'd have to wait quietly and sit still so they wouldn't frighten them. It wasn't long before their patience was rewarded. First one, then a second and a third hummingbird came to feed. They hovered beside the feeders, their wings a blur as they dipped their long thin bills into the openings to get at the sugar water. Two were brilliant red and the third a neon green. They glistened as they bobbed ever so slightly, the light catching their feathers.

"You'll never guess how fast those wings are beating," the guide whispered.

"Thirty times a second," Skye said.

He looked surprised. "Yes!"

"Skye knows her hummingbirds," her mother said.

Skye did know her hummingbirds. They were her favorites because they were so different from any other bird. In some ways, they were almost more like big bumblebees. No other birds could hover. No other birds could fly backward. If most birds were like planes, then hummingbirds were like helicopters.

Skye did dream about being a pilot someday, but not an airplane pilot—a helicopter pilot. She hoped her parents would understand.

As they sat and watched, hummingbirds came, fed and left. They were so quick. Skye thought they were probably bursting with so much life that they couldn't stay still for more than a few seconds. She knew how they felt.

"They look just like the hummingbirds that feed in our backyard," Skye said.

"They could *be* the birds from your backyard," the guide said. "This is where they come to spend their winters."

"All this way?" Skye gasped. "But we flew in a plane for five hours."

"It took them longer, but they flew the same distance," he explained.

"Are you ready to go?" her father asked.

"Can't we stay longer?"

"We can stay all day if you want, but then you'd miss the rest of your surprises."

"The rest?" she asked.

"There are more to come."

# Chapter Six

Led by their guide, Skye and her parents walked deeper into the rainforest. They stopped here and there as Arturo pointed out things they would have missed. He spotted a sloth high up in the crook of a tree. It was a gray lump of fur, sound asleep. The guide explained that sloths slept all day and awoke at night. But even when they were awake, they hardly moved. Arturo said it would be like watching a slow-motion replay on TV to see the sloth ease itself from branch to branch, moving only to find new leaves to dine on.

Occasionally, they passed other people. Some of them wore or carried helmets. Skye wondered what they were for, but she was distracted by the rainforest around her and the upcoming surprises.

Up ahead, through the trees, Skye spotted a building. It was large and unlike any building she'd ever seen. She could almost see through it. It looked like a greenhouse coated in blue-green gauze. It blended into the trees. As they drew closer, Skye thought she saw movement inside the building. Then she realized what she was seeing. Inside the building, hundreds of butterflies fluttered around.

Two sets of doors led to the butterfly garden, so that people coming and going didn't let the butterflies out. Skye walked through the doors. The whole building was alive with butterflies! They floated through the air. They clung to the mesh walls. They clustered on perches that held the pieces of fruit they were feeding on. Their wings shone with brilliant blues and greens.

Skye noticed that the butterflies flew much differently than birds. They seemed to float as much as

they flew. They were so gentle, so fragile. One of the butterflies landed right on Skye's shoulder.

"She must think you're a flower," her father said.

"We have a custom here—if a butterfly lands on you, you get a wish," the guide said.

Then a second butterfly landed right on the top of her head, and a third on her other shoulder.

"Three wishes!" Skye exclaimed.

"I think you must be the luckiest person in the world," Arturo said.

Skye thought about it for a moment. "I am," she said.

"And I guess you're going to get even luckier," her father said. "There's one more surprise to come."

# Chapter Seven

Skye didn't have to wait long to discover her last surprise. A girl wearing a harness and· helmet whizzed by them overhead. She was attached to a long metal cable that ran from one tree to another. As she zoomed along, it looked like her feet were almost touching the treetops. She moved quickly across the top of the building and then disappeared in the trees.

"Is that it?" Skye asked. "Is that what we're going to be doing?"

"Welcome to your last way to fly," her mother said.

* * *

They stood on the tower amid the treetops. It reminded Skye of her tree house back home, except this was much, much higher. And, of course, in her tree house she didn't wear a helmet or a harness. Their instructor had made sure that all of their harnesses were on correctly.

"Remember that the harness will keep you perfectly safe," the instructor said. "You don't even need to hang on, because you can't fall. There's nothing to be afraid of."

"I'm not afraid," Skye said.

The instructor smiled. "I was talking to your parents. Your daughter will be safe."

"We believe you or we wouldn't be here," her father replied.

The guide clicked all of their cables onto the big metal zip-line and told them they were ready to go.

"I'll be waiting for you two at the next tower," her mother said.

Skye's mother stepped off the edge of the tower. The cable sagged, and for a split second she disappeared. Then the cable whirred and she reappeared, flying through the trees. Skye watched as her mother got smaller and smaller in the distance. It looked like she was going to fly forever until she came to a stop at the next treetop tower.

She stood up and gave them a big wave to let them know she was fine. It also signaled that it was Skye's turn to go. Her father checked her harness for the third time. Skye trusted the instructor. She trusted her father. She trusted the harness. Still, she was going to step off a high tower. It wasn't like flying through the ocean or even flying through the sky with a big parachute attached to her back. Here she was in the rainforest, at the very top of one of the tallest trees. She was surrounded by monkeys and birds of all kinds. And she would be higher up than all of them.

Skye stood at the edge of the platform. She looked down along the cable to the next tower, where her mother was waiting.

"Skye," her father said. "You don't have to go."

"I know I don't have to...but I want to."

Skye stepped off the platform. For a second as she dropped, she felt a rush of fear. Then the harness hugged her, and she started sliding down the line. The trees around her were so close that she could almost reach out and touch them. She let go of the cable and spread her arms out as far she could. As she slid, she flapped her arms like they were wings. She was flying!

She zipped along the line, gaining speed as the tower ahead got larger and larger. Her mother, all smiles, was there waiting. She glided right into her mother's arms.

"That was amazing!" Skye said. "I wish I could do it again!"

"Skye, that was only the first zip-line. We have nine more to go," her mother said.

Skye could hardly believe her ears. She gave her mother a gigantic hug. "You really did save the best for last."

# Chapter Eight

Skye set her pencil crayon down with the others. Her creation had taken a lot of work, but not nearly as much as it must have taken her parents to arrange her special surprises. She held the piece up and studied her work. She was happy with it.

Skye left her bedroom and went to the kitchen. Her parents heard the door open and looked up in surprise. They had read her a bedtime story and turned off the lights a long time ago.

"I thought you were asleep," her father said.

"I couldn't sleep because every time I closed my eyes, I saw the rainforest flying by. Besides, I had something I wanted to do."

Skye took the drawing from behind her back and handed it to them. She had drawn pictures of birds, butterflies, baby sea turtles and spider monkeys. She had drawn herself parasailing and her family diving under the ocean and zip-lining through the forest. At the bottom, in big bubble letters, she had written THANK YOU, MOM AND DAD.

"It's beautiful!" her mother said. "This is going right up on the refrigerator."

"Or maybe, because it's so special, we should put it in a frame and hang it on the wall," her father said.

"Before you do that, you have to look at the back," Skye said.

They turned it over. Skye had listed three things.

Bungee jumping

Hang gliding

Skydiving

"Those are my butterfly wishes," she said.

"Those are very exciting things to do," her father said. "But...well..."

48

"You're still too young to do any of those things, I'm afraid," her mother said.

"Sorry," her father added. "You'll have to wait a lot of years before you can have those wishes."

"No, you don't understand," Skye said. "Those aren't for me. Those are my wishes for you!"

"For us?" her mother said.

"That is so nice," her father said.

"I know that you two like to fly even more than I do."

"Are you sure you want to give us your wishes?" her mother asked.

"I'm sure. You already gave me all my wishes."

Skye's father lifted her into his arms. "I already have everything I could ever wish for."

"And more," her mother said as she wrapped her arms around both of them. They had a big family hug.

Skye knew what they meant because she felt the same way too. Flying was wonderful. But not as wonderful as this.

**Eric Walters** began writing in 1993 as a way to entice his grade-five students into becoming more interested in reading and writing. At the end of the year, one student suggested that he try to have his story published. Since that first creation, Eric has published more than eighty novels. Many of his novels have become bestsellers, and he has won over one hundred awards. Often his stories incorporate themes that reflect his background in education and social work and his commitment to humanitarian and social-justice issues. He is a tireless presenter, speaking to more than seventy thousand students per year in schools across the country. Eric is a father of three and lives in Mississauga, Ontario, with his wife, Anita, and dogs Lola and Winnie. For more information, visit www.ericwalters.net.

# Orca Echoes

# Orca Echoes

# Orca Echoes

**Messy Miranda**
*Jeff Szpirglas and Danielle Saint-Onge*
*Illustrated by: Dave Whamond*

**Monster Lunch**
*Pat Skene*
*Illustrated by: Graham Ross*

**Mystery of the Missing Luck**
*Jacqueline Pearce*
*Illustrated by: Leanne Franson*

**Ospreys in Danger**
*Pamela McDowell*
*Illustrated by: Kasia Charko*

**Out and About with the Big Tree Gang**
*Jo Ellen Bogart and Jill Bogart*
*Illustrated by: Dean Griffiths*

**Over the Rainbow with Googol and Googolplex**
*Nelly Kazenbroot*

**The Paper Wagon**
*martha attema*
*Illustrated by: Graham Ross*

**Pirate Island Treasure**
*Marilyn Helmer*
*Illustrated by: David Parkins*

**Prince for a Princess**
*Eric Walters*
*Illustrated by: David Parkins*

**Rhyme Stones**
*Pat Skene*
*Illustrated by: Graham Ross*

**Sam and Nate**
*PJ Sarah Collins*
*Illustrated by: Katherine Jin*

**Sam's Ride**
*Becky Citra*
*Illustrated by: Amy Meissner*

**Saving Sammy**
*By author: Eric Walters*
*Illustrated by: Amy Meissner*

**Sea Dog**
*Dayle Campbell Gaetz*
*Illustrated by: Amy Meissner*

**Seeing Orange**
*Sara Cassidy*
*Illustrated by: Amy Meissner*

**Sharing Snowy**
*Marilyn Helmer*
*Illustrated by: Kasia Charko*

**Skye Above**
*Eric Walters*
*Illustrated by: David Parkins*

**Smuggler's Cave**
*Sonya Spreen Bates*
*Illustrated by: Kasia Charko*

# Orca Echoes